THE
NUFF

Veronica Waldrop
Illustrated By Cat Elliott

TAILWIND PUBLISHING™

For NUFF books, dolls & gear visit
thenuff.com

THE NUFF

Text & Illustrations © 2020 by Will Waldrop

Published by Tailwind Publishing, LLC.
TailwindPublishing.com

ISBN 978-1-7330997-0-7

Executive Producer: Alan Williams

Illustrations: Cat Elliott

Cover and Book Design: Stevie Griffin, steviegriffin.com

Production Management: Della R. Mancuso

Printed in Malaysia
10 9 8 7 6 5 4 3 2

The Nuff is available at discounts for bulk purchases by corporations, institutions, and other organizations. For more information, please contact:
info@tailwindpublishing.com

To Natalia, Nina, and daughters everywhere.
Know that you are *enough*...or a **NUFF**.

Come here, my dears, and listen near.
I have a tale for you

Of a magical being with eyes that shine
and a smile that could light up a room.

I met this child when she was so small,
but instantly I knew

I was made for her and she was made for me.
My love, that child is YOU!

When you arrived in this world,
  the doctor smiled,
    and said in a voice so gruff,

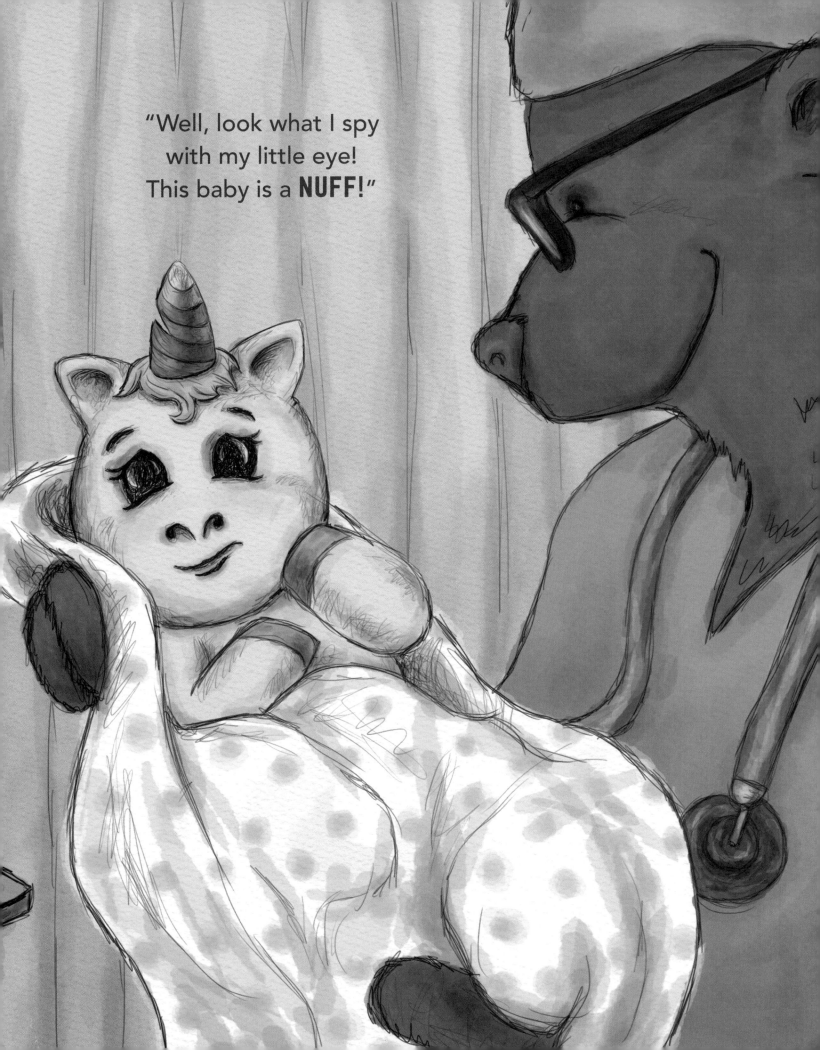

"Well, look what I spy with my little eye! This baby is a **NUFF**!"

"Now what is a **NUFF?**"
You may ask yourself.

So I'm here to fully explain
that a **NUFF** is a strong and beautiful girl
with a powerful heart and brain!

She may not look like the doll in the box
or the girl in the magazine...

But she shines like the sun
with her hair undone,
like a grass-stained summer queen.

A **NUFF** doesn't always wear a dress
or a crown upon her head.

Her hair is sometimes
wild and unruly, in a
pony or piggies instead.

Sometimes she has holes in
the knees of her jeans...
Sometimes she rolls on wheels.

Sometimes a **NUFF** gets dirty,
wearing sneakers not high heels.

Her mind is like a busy beehive,
building dreams and super notions.

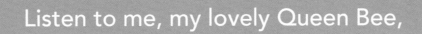

Listen to me, my lovely Queen Bee,

Your soul is as deep as the ocean.

Your heart is like a burning flame
that keeps me warm at night.

When you're kind and strong, you can't go wrong,
even if you're not always right.

Grace is amazing. Perfection is not.
Have faith in who you are.

Just be you and love will shine through,
like a brilliant sparkling star!

Jumping in the mud or splashing in the bath,
my purest joy is hearing you laugh!

So give me a giggle, sing a song, spin and twirl.
Nothing fills my heart like my Nuffy Nuff girl.

When we first met
and I saw your smile,
I figured out what's true.

I looked in the mirror.
Things became clearer.

See! I'm a **NUFF** just like you!

And if you miss the winning goal
or your voice sounds just off key...

Know you are my treasure.
You are enough for me.

When the world says you can't and
you should just give up.
And your path seems rocky and rough...

Know you are brave and beautiful.
You will always be a **NUFF!**

Veronica was selfless and loved to make people laugh.
Throughout her chemotherapy treatments, she spontaneously
wore a unicorn costume around the house to lift the spirits of
her daughters and remind them of the joy they still shared.

In memory of Veronica Waldrop

January 1979 – November 2017

Dear Natalia and Nina,

You are my heartbeat and give me purpose each day. I want this book to be a reminder of how special your mom was. Though we miss her every day, her courage and strength will always live in us. *The Nuff* is a part of our healing and the beginning of a mission to remind you, and daughters everywhere, that *you are enough*.

Laugh, love, and embrace the everyday just as your mom would want you to. You are *fearfully and wonderfully made*, and always remember, you are a NUFF!

Love,
Daddy

From Will Waldrop

I've always said that we see the best of God's love through each other. Through our family's cancer journey, we experienced God's grace through each person who walked beside us. During the toughest of times, this love and care was most redemptive. The prayers and unwavering support allowed us to fight when we thought we had nothing left.

Bill and Gail Waldrop and John and Olga Sparks, I am continually blessed to be surrounded by the best parents and in-laws that anyone could ask for. I admire and respect you so much. You've taught me how to love and lead our family. You epitomize what it means to be selfless through countless acts of unconditional love.

I am eternally grateful to the doctors and medical professionals who cared for Veronica and our family. They showed us that healthcare was much more than a job, but rather a calling. The enduring efforts of these women exemplify the courage and strength of the Nuff. Special thanks to these real-life HEROES: Katherine Castle, MD, Jennifer Connison, RN, Mary C. Raven, MD, and Lauren A. Zatarain.

God brings many blessings in our lives for different reasons, but without question, a bond was meant to be formed with Alan Williams. Alan, thank you for the countless hours of time and energy you and your team have poured into this project. You took an idea and turned it into a movement. Your commitment and vision propelled this book to a place I never dreamed possible.

Betsy Hood, thank you for your commitment to doing whatever it took to make this project successful.

Cat Elliott, thank you for your courage in taking on a new challenge. You created a masterpiece—your passion for the Nuff character shines through on every page. The thoughtfulness and creativity of your work will resonate deeply for many generations to come.

Stevie Griffin, thank you for all of your help and guidance in shaping this wonderful art into a beautiful book.

Thank you Farm Bureau Insurance for walking stride for stride with our family. So many companies call themselves a "family," but this is far from cliché with our organization. I especially want to thank Ronnie Anderson, Blaine Briggs, our sales team, employees, and volunteer leaders. I witnessed firsthand the outpouring of love—prayers, support, teamwork, and inspiration—that picked us up when we needed it the most.

This project would not be possible without Southern Farm Bureau Life Insurance Company. Thanks to the senior management team, the marketing department, and, in particular, David Hurt. David, you saw the significance and long-lasting impact this message could have on so many during a time in my journey where I could barely see anything.